# The Three Little Pigs

## Nick Sharratt      Stephen Tucker

MACMILLAN CHILDREN'S BOOKS

The three little pigs liked living at home
Although the house was small,
But when new babies came along
There just wasn't room for them all.

"It's time we left," the piggies said,
"And built homes of our own."
And as they kissed
    their mum goodbye,
She said, "Be sure to phone."

The pigs set off, and in a field
They saw a heap of straw.
"I'll build my house of that," said one.
"Straw's nice and quick, I'm sure."

The second pig looked all around
And spied a nearby wood.
"I'll build my house of sticks," he squeaked.
"Sticks are really good."

"To build a house," the third pig said,
"I know the thing to choose.
Not straw or sticks, but solid bricks.
Yes, they're the things to use."

And carefully he laid his bricks
One by one by one.
He built four walls and then the roof.
At last his work was done.

Now close by was another house
And a big bad wolf lived there.
His fridge was very empty,
His cupboards were quite bare.

The wolf had eaten all the food
(That's why he was so big).
"I fancy something else," he said.
"And what I'd like is pig!"

He went to see his neighbour
In his nice new house of straw.
But the piggy saw him coming,
Ran inside and locked the door.

Said wolf, "If you don't let me in,
Then I shall huff and puff
And blow your house down."
    Which he did.
And one puff was enough!

He chased the piggies down the lane,
And would have caught them, but . . .
Their brother shouted,
"In here, quick!"
Then slammed the
        front door shut.

"Now I've got you,"
        l▓▓hed the wolf.
"▓▓▓▓▓ke very long
To▓▓▓▓ little house down, too!"
But this time he was wrong.

No matter how he huffed and puffed
The wolf just couldn't make
This house fall down.
    The walls stood firm.
They didn't even shake.

"I don't give up that easily,"
The sly wolf growled. "Oh no.
I'll climb onto the roof
And down the chimney I shall go!"

"Coming to get you," called the wolf,
"Whether you're ready or not."
He slithered down the chimney
And landed in a pot . . .

. . . Which was full of salty water,
Onions, carrots, too.
The piggies cheered, "Hip, hip, hooray!
The wolf is in a stew!"

First published 2001 by Macmillan Children's Books
This edition published 2009 by Macmillan Children's Books
a division of Macmillan Publishers Limited
20 New Wharf Road, London N1 9RR
Basingstoke and Oxford
Associated companies throughout the world
www.panmacmillan.com

ISBN: 978-0-230-73613-9

7 9 8 6

A CIP catalogue record for this book is available from the British Library.

Printed in Malaysia by Tien Wah Press